THE SASQUATCH AND THE LUMBERJACK

CRIX SHERIDAN

little bigfoot
an imprint of sasquatch books
seattle, wa

PICK

ROAST

For Rouen. May the journey abound with peace, joy, and grace.

Manufactured in China by C&C Offset Printing Co. Ltd. Shenzhen, Guangdong Province, in January 2018

Published by Little Bigfoot, an imprint of Sasquatch Books

22 21 20 19 18   9 8 7 6 5 4 3 2 1

Editors: Ben Clanton, Christy Cox | Production editor: Bridget Sweet | Design: Anna Goldstein

Library of Congress Cataloging-in-Publication Data
Names: Sheridan, Crix, author, illustrator.
Title: The sasquatch and the lumberjack / Crix Sheridan.
Description: Seattle, WA : Little Bigfoot, an imprint of Sasquatch Books,
    [2018]. | Summary: Illustrations and sparse text reveal a developing
    friendship between a sasquatch and a lumberjack, from their first meeting
    through a year of apple picking, skiing, hiking, and swimming.
Identifiers: LCCN 2017041455 | ISBN 9781632171610 (hardback)
Subjects: | CYAC: Friendship--Fiction. | Sasquatch--Fiction. |
    Loggers--Fiction. | BISAC: JUVENILE FICTION / Action & Adventure /
    General. | JUVENILE FICTION / Social Issues / Friendship.
Classification: LCC PZ7.1.S5155 Sas 2018 | DDC [E]--dc23
LC record available at https://lccn.loc.gov/2017041455
ISBN: 978-1-63217-161-0

Sasquatch Books | 1904 Third Avenue, Suite 710 | Seattle, WA 98101
(206) 467-4300 | SasquatchBooks.com

CRIX SHERIDAN is an illustrator, storyteller, and designer hailing from east of the Rockies and west of the Atlantic. He has a degree in film and writing, and visual communication. His graphic novels include *Motorcycle Samurai*, *Spacebat and the Fugitives*, and *The TroubleMakers*. This is his first children's book. He currently lives in Seattle with his wife, baby boy, and their two and a half bikes.